Date Due

Jessica and the Wolf

A Story for Children Who Have Bad Dreams

by Ted Lobby, M.S.W.

illustrated by Tennessee Dixon

MAGINATION PRESS · NEW YORK

For Mackenzie, Rita and Sam

Library of Congress Cataloging-in-Publication Data

Lobby, Ted
Jessica and the wolf : a story for children who have bad dreams /
by Ted Lobby : illustrated by Tennessee Dixon.
p. cm.
Summary: With her parents' support, Jessica finds the strength and
self-reliance to conquer a recurring bad dream.
ISBN 0-945354-22-3. — ISBN 0-945354-21-5 (pbk.)
[1. Nightmares — Fiction. 2. Dreams — Fiction. 3. Self-reliance-
— Fiction.] I. Dixon, Tennessee, ill. II. Title.
PZ7.L7789Je 1990
[E] — dc20 89-29688
CIP
AC

 Published by Magination Press, an Imprint of Brunner/Mazel, Inc., 19 Union Square West, New York, NY 10003

Paperback edition distributed to the trade by Publishers Group West, 4065 Hollis St., Emeryville, CA 94608
Telephone 800-365-3453; in CA call collect 415-658-3453

Distributed in Canada by Book Center, 1140 Beaulac St., Montreal, Quebec H4R 1R8, Canada

Manufactured in the United States of America

10 9 8 7 6 5 4 3 2 1

Introduction for Parents

Everyone has bad dreams. Everyone's children have bad dreams. When our children cry out in the night, we each have special ways of comforting them. Probably we kiss and hug and sit with our children for a while. Maybe we bring them into the safety of our bed for the rest of the night. Or sing a lullaby. Or offer a glass of milk.

These techniques work fine most of the time. But when a nightmare persists, something more may be needed.

The parents in this story help their child solve her problem of a recurring bad dream. They help her use her nightmare as an opportunity to learn. She learns that her parents are there to help her when she needs help. She learns that with a little help from others, she can help herself. She also learns self-reliance and pride in her own abilities. Working together with her parents and trusting in herself, she transforms a painful episode into a positive experience.

You, too, can use the method portrayed in the story with your child. The most important part of this method is talking about the thing that is scary and working together in an atmosphere of respect and trust. Your task is to draw out your child's own ideas about how to solve the problem. This is also a good way to solve many kinds of problems with children and with other people!

Bad dreams may be simple, one-time scary dreams, recurring nightmares, or night terrors. Any of these may be normal childhood experiences. The nightmare in this story was rather easily solved by the child's increased confidence in herself. But sometimes a wolf or other frightening figure in a dream can represent a real person or situation that is directly threatening or harming a child in daily life. If talking and planning with your child does not succeed in making bad dreams go away, you may want to ask a qualified professional to help you all solve the problem together.

Jessica tosses and turns. She kicks her feet. She rolls around. She calls out, “Go away.” Jessica is having a bad dream.

A wolf is chasing her.

The wolf is sleek and silver.

It runs swiftly, with smooth, long strides.

Jessica's legs are getting tired.

She hears the wolf's rumbling growl.

The wolf is getting closer.

Jessica screams and wakes up. Her mom and dad also wake up.

"She's having another bad dream," says Mom.

"Maybe we can help her make the bad dreams stop," says Dad.

They both put on their robes and hurry to Jessica's room.

"I'm scared," says Jessica. "I want the dreams to stop."

Mom hugs her tightly and says, "We can help you, honey."

"You know, sweetie," says Dad, "dreams are not real. They seem real, though. And sometimes they can be very scary. But there are some things you can do so you won't be so afraid."

"Like what?" asks Jessica.

"The first thing," says Mom, "is talking. Talking about a scary thing helps make it less scary. You can start by telling us about your dream."

Jessica takes a deep breath and says, "There's a big mean wolf chasing me. . ."

When Jessica finishes, her mom says, "Great job! Now we need to figure out a plan."

"What do you mean, plan?" asks Jessica.

"A plan is the first thing you need to make a problem go away," explains Mom.

"Like what thing?" asks Jessica, trying to understand.

"Since it is your dream," says Dad, "your plan can be anything you want."

"I want the wolf to go away," says Jessica quickly.

"How would you like to get rid of that wolf?" asks Dad.

A big grin spreads across Jessica's face. "Magic!" she says.

"What kind of magic will you do?" asks Mom.

"First I need a magic wand. Can I get one?" Jessica asks hopefully.

"We can make one tomorrow," says Dad. "And you can make up some magic words to give it special powers."

"What if I get scared?" asks Jessica.

"What do you usually do when you are afraid?" asks Mom.

"I try to be brave and I hug Sarah," says Jessica, hugging her favorite bear. "Can Sarah help, too?"

"That's a good idea," says Dad. "If you get scared, just give Sarah a squeeze."

"Now it's time for you and Sarah to go back to sleep," says Mom. "I don't think that wolf will bother you again tonight. Tomorrow we'll finish making the plan."

At bedtime the next night, Jessica has her magic wand ready.

"What are your magic words?" asks Mom.

"Bibbedy, Bobbedy, Beebee," giggles Jessica.

"And where is Sarah?" asks Dad.

"Right here!" says Jessica.

"Good," says Mom. "Here's the plan: First, remember that the dream is not real and the wolf is imaginary. You can use your magic wand to change your dream. When the wolf gets close, stop running and turn around. If you get nervous give Sarah a hug. That's what friends are for, to help when you need it. Then say your magic words, and swing your magic wand, and command that wolf to BE GONE! Okay? Ready to give it a try?"

"I think so," says Jessica.

Mom and Dad give Jessica a kiss and say goodnight.

Jessica can't fall asleep, so she decides to practice. She gets out of bed and stands holding Sarah in one hand and the wand in the other.

"I hope I can do it," she says, swinging the wand.

"Bibbedy, Bobbedy, Beebee. Wolf, you go away," she whispers.

"I don't think I can do it," she says, feeling little and scared.

Then she gives Sarah a big squeeze. She takes a deep breath. She swings the wand in a big circle. And she says,

"BIBBEDY, BOBBEDY, BEEBEE.
I COMMAND YOU TO BE GONE!"

She is surprised how loud and strong her voice sounds. "Maybe I *can* do it," she thinks. She climbs into bed feeling much braver. "I know I can," she says out loud.

She has a plan, some magic, and Sarah. She turns onto her tummy, closes her eyes, and soon she's asleep.

The dream begins again.

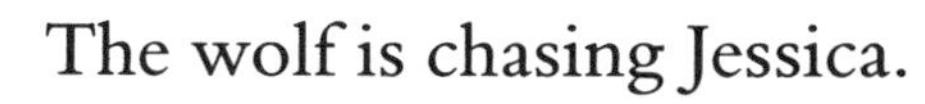
The wolf is chasing Jessica.

She hears its deep growl.

She runs as fast as she can.

The wolf is very close when Jessica stops. She turns around and faces the wolf. She swings her wand in a big circle and says in a loud strong voice, "BIBBEDY, BOBBEDY, BEEBEE. I COMMAND YOU TO BE GONE!"

For a moment nothing happens. Jessica hugs Sarah tightly.

Then, suddenly, the wolf is gone.

Jessica looks at Sarah.
She says, "Wow, that was scary!
But we did it anyway."

She sighs, taps her wand, hugs Sarah,
and sleeps peacefully the rest of the night.

The next morning, Jessica can't wait to tell her parents what happened. She and Sarah charge into their room and jump into their bed.

"What's this?" asks Dad, rubbing the sleep from his eyes.

"I did it. It worked!" Jessica tells them excitedly.

Mom and Dad together hug Jessica and Sarah. "What a kid!" says Dad. Jessica feels very proud.

Sometimes Jessica still has bad dreams. They don't scare her much anymore, though. She knows that with some help, a plan, a little magic, and a friend, bad dreams can be changed.